SNOW PLACE TO GO

Samantha Baca

Contents

One

Tiffany

"Hi, I'm checking in," I said to the woman with curly red hair that was pulled into a ponytail with a ribbon wrapped around it. I would probably think she was a cheerleader if it weren't for the bifocals that she had on. She leaned closer to the computer, typing something on the keyboard before she looked up at me.

"What's the name, dear?" she asked, her voice soft like my grandmother's.

"Tiffany Thompson."

I glanced over at the man who had been standing behind me, who was now being helped by the other receptionist. The only reason I knew it was a man was from his brash phone conversation that took place the entire time I waited in line.

I imagined an older man— someone powerful and

aggressive based on how he was speaking to people. Instead, I found that he was actually younger— maybe a few years older than me, and quite attractive. His dress slacks and crisp, white button-down shirt didn't mesh well with the log cabin and lumberjack vibe of the other men who were running around, but it suited him well.

I listened to their conversation shamelessly while the woman in front of me struggled to get her computer to work.

"Your name, sir?"

"Luke Lane."

A few clicks on her keyboard, and she had his reservation pulled up.

She was younger— probably twenty years younger than the woman helping me, and seemed much more comfortable with technology.

"Alright, I show that you'll be staying in cabin 6. It's outside, around the corner, the last cabin on the left."

I let out a soft sigh, wishing this would move faster and that I could be on my way too.

"Okay, dear, I show that you'll be in Cabin 6. Let me get your key."

She turned around and reached for the key at the same time the other girl did. They both pulled back then frowned when they realized that it was the only set of keys left on the pegboard, and there were two separate people checking in.

"That's my key, dear," she said to the other woman, her hand slightly trembling as she reached up for it.

"I don't think so," the other girl replied. "I show cabin six on his reservation, and that's this key."

"Mine shows cabin six as well."

"Mind if I take a look?"

I exchanged glances with the attractive stranger beside me, wondering what in the world was going on. Surely, there had to be some sort of error in their computer system and another key lying around somewhere.

They stood at her computer, confirming the information for my reservation before turning to the other one and checking his. Finally, the younger woman looked at us and held her hands together in a peace offering.

"I'm sorry," she said firmly. "It appears that there's been a mistake, and both of you have been assigned the same cabin."

"That's fine, I'll just take another one," I replied, waving my hand dismissively.

"Unfortunately, there aren't any. We're completely booked with it being five days before Christmas. This is the last cabin that we have available."

I closed my eyes and pinched the bridge of my nose. This was just my luck with everything else I had going on. *Why wouldn't I be able to escape for the holidays and hide away in a cabin in the middle of nowhere?*

"We can add a rollaway bed to the cabin, free of charge for the inconvenience," she added nervously, looking between us for an answer.

"You're suggesting that we *share* the cabin?" Luke said, speaking for the first time since this whole debacle started.

"I would strongly encourage it. There's a storm moving in that will shut down all of the roads to and from the cabin for a few days. There's no way to make it down the mountain safely before it hits." She paused for a moment, letting this news sink in. "Our one bedroom cabins are very spacious and can easily accommodate two guests," she assured.

He let out the breath that I had been holding as we sighed heavily together.

"I'm fine with sleeping on the rollaway bed in the living room if you're okay with sharing the cabin," he offered, turning to face me.

I felt my cheeks blush, feeling his curious dark gray eyes watch me.

"Sure, that works for me," I choked out. "As long as there is a separate bathroom and bedroom, that's fine."

"Perfect," the girl said, holding the key out between the two of us.

He reached forward and took it, giving me a tight smile, before reaching down to grab his luggage.

"The dining hall is open until seven pm and will open again at six tomorrow morning. Your cabin is fully stocked with extra linens, however, you can call the main desk if there's anything else you might need. We're honored to have you stay at Bear Creek and hope you enjoy your stay."

I turned on my heel, pulling my suitcase behind me as I struggled to keep the duffle bag and my purse from sliding off. Luke led the way out, holding the door open for me as we stepped out into a bitter gust of wind. I covered my mouth with my hand, trying to shield myself as it took my breath away. He looked around, his eyes narrowed and focused, before he set off in the direction of our cabin.

It was a short walk but felt longer with the ankle-deep snow covering the ground. I was thankful that I had packed accordingly. It was a very purposeful plan—rent a cabin in the woods, watch the snow fall while cuddled up under a blanket with a good book, and blame getting snowed in as the reason why I couldn't make it home for Christmas with my family.

It had *nothing* to do with the fact that I was the oldest of my parent's four kids and the only one who was still single and childless. I was reminded of it *every single year* during the holidays when my mom would moan and complain about how she wished I would find someone to settle down with. *You're not a spring chicken anymore, Tiffany. Men don't want women the same when they're in their thirties. The clock is ticking, you better start looking.*

That was a few years ago, right after my thirtieth birthday. Nothing had changed since then other than the number of extra prayers my mom said for my poor eggs that would never be fertilized while I blew out the thirty-two candles on my cake. It felt juvenile to have a cake that was basically *on fire*, but she wanted to make sure that I didn't forget just how old I was or how much harder it was to do things—like blowing out candles—the older that I got.

Once we found our cabin, he fumbled with the key until it

finally turned and opened into a cute, rustic-looking room. We walked inside and closed the door, keeping the cold out as he turned on the rest of the lights. It wasn't a huge cabin but had plenty of room for us to move around each other without getting in the way.

The living room and kitchen were all one room, divided by a breakfast bar that extended past the sink. Cream-colored paint covered the walls, making it look more open and homier. I was relieved that it wasn't over the top with log walls like the main area where we had checked in. This was calmer, more relaxing.

I set my luggage down by the couch, out of the way, and walked around, taking in the views from the oversized windows that framed the living room. The room darkening curtains were pulled back with sheer curtains covering the panes. Off to the side of the room was a large, plush chair that would be the perfect spot to sit down and read.

A decent-sized tv hung mounted to the wall above an entertainment center that was fully stocked with board games and DVDs. There were plenty of places to sit with the loveseat and sofa taking up the majority of the space around the dark gray wood coffee table.

I was walking to the back of the cabin to check out the bathroom and bedroom, when there was a knock on the door. Luke nodded and walked over to answer it, while I continued with my tour. The bathroom was spacious, with a double vanity and a large mirror that stretched the width of the counter. There was a walk-in shower that was easily big enough to fit two people, accompanied by one of those fancy shower heads that has twenty-some different water pressure options. Beside it was an inviting tub with an assortment of soaking salts and bath bombs lining the shelf behind it.

The door closed, and I felt the gush of cold air rush in as I went back to the living room. The rollaway bed had been delivered, along with a bottle of wine—compliments of the manager for our inconvenience. The bed in the back was a king and looked plenty big to fit both of us comfortably, but I was too nervous to suggest that. If needed, I could sleep on the other bed until he left—which reminded me that I didn't know how long we were going to be shacked up together.

"So, I checked the closet in the bedroom, and it's pretty big if you wanted to share it," I said awkwardly, unsure of what else to say.

"Thanks, I don't think I'll have much use for it. I won't be here that long."

"Oh?" I blurted out, feeling the heat of embarrassment wash over me.

"I'm only here through Christmas. I'll be checking out the day after."

Of course, he is.

"I'm leaving the same day."

It felt like a stupid thing to say since he hadn't bothered to ask.

"Well, I'll take the rollaway bed. You can have the bedroom and the closet."

"I don't mind—"

"I insist," he interrupted firmly. Just like that, it was the same cold, harsh tone that I had heard earlier when he was on the phone.

"Okay, thank you," I mumbled, walking over to grab my suitcase.

I went to the bedroom and closed the door, needing some space from the mysterious man on the other side of the wall.

Two

Luke

There were plenty of things in life that I didn't like, and surprises were one of them. When they informed me that there was a mix-up with their system, I would have normally raised my voice and demanded that they fix it— immediately. But the beautiful blonde-haired woman next to me with the sparkling green eyes had me agreeing to share a cabin with her, just so I could see her again.

I didn't even care that I had spent my entire holiday bonus to rent a cabin up here at the last minute and was now stuck sleeping on a rickety rollaway bed instead of the comfortable king bed with the plush pillow-top mattress. It was worth the sacrifice, as I watched her move around the space, her curiosity about me as high as mine was about her.

When she offered to sleep in the living room on the crappy bed, I scoffed and tried to decline as politely as I could. That didn't mean that it didn't come out gruff—just that I tried. There was no way in hell that I was going to let it happen. I was raised better than that, even if I was currently avoiding any and *all* interaction with my family right now.

She had been in the bedroom for over an hour before the door opened, and she walked out, wearing a thick wool coat and a beanie.

"I'm heading over to the main hall to grab dinner. Did you want to join me?"

I realized that it was already after six, and if I wanted to eat tonight, this was probably my last chance.

"Sure, let me grab my coat."

I had taken the opportunity to change while she was in the bedroom and traded my work attire for a pair of jeans and a ribbed fitted sweater. I pulled on my coat and then grabbed the key from the table before heading out into the cold with her.

The dining hall was surprisingly busy with other guests milling around, chatting as they added food to their plates from the buffet. I had assumed that there would be a formal dining experience with a menu and waiters, but apparently, I was wrong.

We checked in with the hostess and took the number that she gave us to an empty table before heading over to the food. I stepped back and let her go first, smiling as I held my hand out in front of me for her to pass. She grabbed a plate and walked down the side, leaning forward to get a better look at the salad options in front of her.

I picked up a plate and wandered over to the meats. The selection didn't look that great, and I assumed it was because they were getting ready to close down soon and weren't planning on making anything fresh. I chose a grilled chicken breast and loaded my plate with a side of mashed potatoes and a cob of corn before returning to the table.

Tiffany was already sitting there, picking at her salad with her fork. I was surprised that she didn't get anything else, but then again, her plate didn't look like it needed anything else. There were so many vibrant colors, from the dark green of the spinach to the orange carrot sticks and deep red tomatoes—it looked like something you would see on one of those fancy cooking shows.

"That's quite the salad," I commented, pulling out the chair across from her and sitting down.

"Thank you. There weren't a ton of options, so I worked with what I had."

"Yeah, I agree. I'm hoping that there's a better selection in the morning."

"I'm sure there will be. It's hard this close to closing time, they don't want to waste food by cooking fresh items when there's still stuff that hasn't been eaten."

I smiled and studied her as I cut into my chicken and took a bite.

"You seem to know a lot about how restaurants work," I noted after I swallowed my bite.

While we were gone, the waitress had come by and left glasses of ice water on the table for us. I took a drink, washing down the somewhat dry chicken.

"I'm a chef," she shrugged as if it were no big deal.

"Oh yeah?" I asked, wiping my face with a napkin and leaning back against the metal seat. "Where at?"

"A little café, just south of the Oregon state line."

"So, what brought you to Bear Creek?"

She paused for a moment, taking a bite before she answered.

"I wanted to spend the holiday snowed in somewhere. If I

were snowed in, then I'd have no place to go," she giggled nervously.

"Or *snow* place to go," I joked, smiling when she laughed at my corny attempt to be funny.

"What about you?" she asked. "What brought you to the middle of nowhere, five days before Christmas?"

"Family."

Her eyes widened as she looked around the room.

"Oh, are you joining your family up here for the holiday?"

I was mid-chew when she asked, which caused my food to get stuck in my throat when I tried to swallow. I started choking, reaching for the glass of water before I caused a scene.

"No," I choked in between drinks. "I'm here to avoid seeing my family. As far as they're concerned, I'm working and can't make it home."

"Where's home?"

"Cedar Plank, Nebraska."

"Why don't you want to see your family?"

I felt my hands start sweating from the constant questions, suddenly feeling like I was being interrogated.

"Because they're incredibly judgmental, and I never live up to their expectations," I said gruffly. "Are you here because you want a Hallmark Christmas, or are you here to avoid your family too?"

"You caught me," she laughed, the sound of it sending a warm feeling straight to my heart. She covered her mouth with her hand and continued to giggle.

"I knew it," I teased. "No one wants to willingly get snowed in somewhere."

"That's not true," she objected, pointing her fork in my direction. "I would very much love to get snowed in somewhere. No responsibilities other than relaxing and watching the snow fall—it would be so wonderful."

"Okay, *maybe* if there were no responsibilities. But where I come from, you never get away from them, so it wouldn't be a realistic option for me."

"Well, that's unfortunate," she said, her eyes narrowing as she focused on me. When the light hit them just right, I could see small brown flecks mixed in with the emerald green, and it was hypnotizing.

"That's the same thing my parents always say," I muttered under my breath while poking at my chicken with the fork.

"So, why are you avoiding your family?"

She popped a piece of spinach in her mouth and chewed as she waited for me to answer.

"Because I can't handle *another* holiday of them riding my ass about my life choices."

She pulled her head back, and her jaw dropped open.

"I thought I was the only one with parents like that."

"Nope," I laughed. "I can guarantee that mine are probably *the worst*."

"Okay, let's see," she said, her eyes filled with mischief.

"See what?"

"Whose parents are worse. We'll compare battle stories and then decide."

"I don't think you know what you're getting yourself into," I warned playfully. "Unfortunately, I will always win at this game."

"We'll just see about that," she retorted. "I'll even let you go first."

I pushed my plate to the side and folded my hands in front of me on the table.

"Fine. My parents tell everyone they meet that I'm gay when I'm not."

"What?!" she gasped. "Why would they do that?"

"Because they don't want to believe that I've intentionally stayed single. Plus, I'm a wedding planner in Los Angeles and work with a lot of LGBTQIA clients."

"Wow," she said, nodding in disbelief.

"Your turn."

"Well, my mom tried to marry me off to the new guy in town, right after the Sunday service at church. When she heard that he was a doctor, she made sure to tell him that she thought my eggs were getting too old and dried up and asked if he wouldn't mind taking a look."

I choked on the drink of water I had just taken, embarrassed that it was the second time to happen in under an hour. *What was wrong with me?*

"That's pretty bad, but you still don't win. My mom actually created a profile for me on a men's only dating site. She even attempted to photoshop my driver's license photo to a beach scene she found online. It was a terrible picture. I hurt her feelings even more when I told her that gay men would not be impressed by it and that she was dooming me to stay single."

She tossed her head back and laughed, her blond hair cascading down her back.

"I'm sure that got her even more riled up."

"That it did," I chuckled.

"So because you're a wedding planner, you're automatically gay?" she questioned, leaning forward and resting her elbows on the table.

"It would seem so. I guess it doesn't help that I've *never* taken a woman home to meet my family, and unlike my siblings, I choose to keep my personal details just that— personal."

"How many siblings do you have?"

"I have four sisters. Two older and two younger, which leaves me as the middle child, and of course, the only boy."

"Man, this just keeps getting better," she giggled, covering her mouth.

"See, I told you—I win."

"Not so fast," she countered. "Gay wedding planner isn't that bad. If anything—I would say it's pretty damn good, because I would totally hire you to plan my wedding, knowing that you would have every detail on point, and it would be perfect."

"Oh, so now I'm planning your wedding?" I teased, enjoying the playful banter between us.

"Yeah, once I find someone willing to marry me," she snorted and rolled her eyes. "I have to beat them away with a bat, there's so many lined up."

"I'm sure it's not that bad," I said softly, sensing the hurt in her tone.

"It's not that I want to stay single—even though my mother would say otherwise. I just haven't found *the one*. I'm only thirty-two, why should I settle?"

"I'm thirty-eight and still refuse to settle. I don't think there's a damn thing wrong with you waiting for the right person."

She smiled, but it fell flat before it reached her eyes, the sadness overshadowing it.

"So, what made you decide to be a chef?" I asked, shifting the conversation to something lighter.

"I've always had a love for food—as you can see," she said shyly, extending her arms for me to see her body. "At one point, my mom tried to get me to enlist in the army so I would stay away from food. She said *maybe if you had a job where you were physically active and not constantly around food, then you wouldn't have to worry about your addiction.*"

"Addiction?" I asked, raising an eyebrow. She was curvy and in the best way. Not overweight like her mother seemed to imply.

"She thinks that I'm addicted to food."

I looked down at her salad, wondering if she was eating it because she wanted to or because she held this heavy guilt that her mom loaded onto her.

"I don't see anything wrong with what you're eating," I muttered. "And I don't see a damned thing wrong with your body either—just for the record. Curves are sexy, and I like a woman who wears them proudly."

"Well, thank you, I appreciate your gay insight," she teased with a wink. "But trust me—I like to eat. I'm a meat and potatoes kind of gal. I want savory foods with robust flavors that burst on your tongue. I only got salad tonight because it looked like the safest option out of what was left."

I felt my lips turning up into a smile. It had been a while since I was able to talk to a woman and have it stay this lighthearted and fun. I didn't date much because it was hard to meet women close to my age who weren't talking about ticking biological clocks and pressuring me for a second date before the check came.

"That's impressive," I commented, meaning it. "My job requires me to have a broad palate, and honestly, I enjoy when I get roped into food tastings."

"I bet it's a lot of fun, getting to meet so many new people and plan weddings. I've always wanted to get into catering so that I could network and get out more. Plus, growing up in a large family trained me to know how to cook for large groups."

"Why don't you do it then?"

"Do what?"

"Catering."

"Oh," her face fell. "I don't know. I guess I've just never

had the opportunity. Most people want to hire someone with years of experience, so it makes it hard to get your foot in the door."

"What about the place you currently work? Do they do any catering services that you could help out with?"

She paused for a moment, taking a drink of water before she set the glass down on the table with a shaky hand.

"I'm actually in between jobs right now."

"Oh, I'm sorry," I apologized.

"It's okay. I'm taking a few weeks off to rest and recuperate, and then I plan to hit the ground running on January first to find something new. It's a great opportunity to find something that I really want to do and start over."

"Well, here's to new opportunities," I said, raising my glass. She lifted hers, and they clinked in the air.

Three

Tiffany

I didn't know if it was possible to be colder outside when we left the dining hall than it was when we first went over there. It felt like the temperature dropped at least twenty degrees which made the falling snow feel like shards of glass that poked at my face which was already stinging from the gusts of wind that had whipped past us.

Once we got to our cabin, we rushed inside and locked the door. I pulled off my coat and hung it on the back of the kitchen chair, rubbing my hands together to warm myself up. Luke worked on starting the fireplace before taking off his coat and hanging it next to mine. I curled up on the couch and tucked my legs under me, thinking back to dinner.

I had expected Luke to have some sort of comment about my body or how I needed to eat more salad, but he surprised me when he said that he liked a woman who had curves and wore them with confidence. The one thing that I didn't have was confidence, but he hadn't caught onto that yet.

The flames of the fire danced across the walls, making me feel more relaxed. I hadn't thought much about what we would do or how we would share this space. Then, realizing that I was technically in his bedroom, I started to worry that I should move to my room and give him some space.

I got up and folded the blanket, hanging it over the edge of the couch while he was in the bathroom. I was on my way to the room when the door opened, and we almost collided in the hallway.

"Sorry," I laughed, stepping to the side. "I was just heading to the room so you could have some space."

His dark eyes narrowed at me before he said, "you're fine, I don't need space."

I paused, unsure of where to go. I wasn't ready for bed yet, but I also didn't want him to feel obligated to spend more time with me.

"I saw some board games, did you want to play one?" he asked, lingering beside me.

"Sure, that sounds great." My voice was quieter than usual, straining to come out.

I followed him back to the living room and sat on the couch while he scanned the options.

"We have Battleship, Monopoly, or Clue. The rest I've never heard of unless you have the desire to play Mall Madness."

He arched a brow. I chewed my lower lip and giggled.

"Oh, I totally have the desire to play Mall Madness," I snickered.

He sighed dramatically, letting his head fall to his chest. He ran a hand through his dark hair and then muttered, "I knew I shouldn't have mentioned that one."

"Hey, you're just afraid that I might know more about shopping than a *gay wedding planner*," I teased as he grabbed it from the shelf and brought it over.

"Do you want to play on the couch, or should we move to the floor and use the coffee table?"

"Honestly, if I get down on the floor, you probably won't get me up again," I joked, knowing how much truth there was to it.

"Fair enough, I don't know that my knees could handle it either."

I scooted to the end of the couch and helped him set the game up in the middle between us.

"Do you know how to play this, or should I read the directions?" he asked once everything was out of the box.

"Please, I grew up in the eighties. I don't need no stinkin' directions," I laughed.

Twenty minutes later, we were staring at the board, unsure of what to do next.

"Are you sure that we don't need to read the directions," he teased, smirking at the confused look on my face.

"No, I just need to concentrate."

"On a shopping game for ages nine and up?"

"I need the sound," I whined. "I can't play without hearing where the sales are."

"Okay," he said. "I can fix that."

He jumped up and walked over to the entertainment center, grabbing the handful of remotes and bringing them back to the couch. A few minutes later, he was swapping batteries and the game came to life.

"There's a sale at the record store," the voice said.

I squealed and clapped my hands excitedly.

"Alright, now it's on," I taunted.

"I thought it was supposed to be on from the moment we started," he countered. "It seems like maybe my internal gay guy does know a thing or two about shopping after all."

I rolled my eyes and took my turn after pressing the button to start the game. I already had three of the six items that I needed to purchase, while Luke had four. I looked at the cash that I still had on hand and knew that I would have to stop by the bank unless I could hit one of the sales on the way to the parking lot.

Luke reached the record store before I could and added another item to his purchases. I was feeling the tension, knowing that he was probably going to win after all. The next sale ended up being at the pet shop, which I was standing right in front of. I smiled as I swiped my card to pay for my purchase, giggling at the gargled sound the game made from years of use and abuse.

We were neck to neck, in the final stretch, both sitting with five purchases and heading toward the parking lot while trying to get the last item on our list.

I tapped my finger nervously against my chin as I waited for my turn. There was a clearance sale at the fashion boutique, but it would force me to move away from the parking lot in order to get to it. I didn't have enough money to purchase anything else along the way.

Luke headed into the store to grab his last purchase and covered his face with his hands when he realized that he didn't have enough money to make it. He was in the same position now, and either had to head back to the ATM to take out cash, or he had to get to the same clearance sale that I was closer to.

He scrunched his face and glared at me as he ended his turn and watched me win the game. I laughed at the sour expression, knowing that he must be a sore loser.

"Wanna go again?" I asked, making my girl dance her way out to the parking lot.

"No way," he laughed. "That was brutal enough."

I leaned against the couch and laughed with him. It had been fun, but I had to admit that I was pleasantly surprised to see how invested he had gotten in the game.

"Well, I guess I shall leave you to dwell on your loss," I teased. "It's getting late, and I'm sure you want to get some rest."

He hesitated for a moment, a look of uncertainty on his face.

"I was thinking about watching a movie if you wanted to join me?"

I noticed how his eyes seemed to beg me to stay even though he didn't say it.

"Sure, that would be nice. I'll see if there's some popcorn in the kitchen."

I got up and walked into the kitchen, wondering who this man really was. The cold, demanding man I had heard on the phone earlier was now replaced with a nice, gentle one who didn't seem to want to be alone.

32

Four

Luke

I sat next to her on the couch, sharing a giant bowl of popcorn while we watched Top Gun. I had assumed that she would pick a chick flick when I gave her the option, so color me surprised when she went for a classic. It was getting late, and I knew that the movie would be over soon, but I didn't want my time with her to end.

It wasn't like I didn't enjoy being alone—hell, I preferred it over most people's company. But there was something different about her that made me desperate to hang out with her. It was like she was a magnet, and I couldn't escape the pull toward her. Maybe it was because she was the first person I had talked to in a long time that was genuine and cared about what I had to say. She didn't just humor me and listen to my stories. She made eye contact and gave me her undivided attention as if I was the most interesting person she'd ever talked to.

I shifted on the couch, relaxing against the soft leather as I considered sleeping on it instead of the rollaway bed they brought earlier. That thing looked like it had seen better days, and I was pretty confident that I would wake up tomorrow stiff and sore from a poor night's sleep.

The not so gentle sound of snoring escaped from Tiffany's mouth as her head fell to the side, sound asleep. I fought the urge to pick her up and carry her to the bedroom, knowing how inappropriate that would be given that she barely knew me. Instead, I cleaned up our snacks and carried our glasses to the kitchen before grabbing a blanket and covering her. I gave in and set up the other bed, wincing as it creaked under my weight, afraid that it would wake her up.

I was just getting settled in when I rolled over and saw her eyes flutter open. She sat up and looked around the room, finally finding me in the dark after her eyes adjusted. I had left the light on in the bathroom with the door cracked to give off a small amount of light so she didn't freak out if she woke up in the middle of the night to a pitch-black room that she wasn't familiar with.

"What time is it?" she asked sleepily.

"Just after midnight," I replied, rolling onto my side and propping myself up on my elbow. "You were in a deep sleep, so I didn't want to wake you."

"Was I snoring?"

"Not that I could tell," I lied, not knowing if it would embarrass her if I said yes.

"You're a terrible liar," she laughed. "But I'm going to head to bed and let you get some rest. Are you sure you don't want to switch and take the bedroom?"

"No," I said sternly. "I want you to sleep in the room. I'll be fine out here."

"Okay, thank you. Good night."

"Good night."

Once she was in her room, I waited until I heard the door locked and let out a sigh of relief. As much as I wanted to spend time with her, I was thankful that she was smart enough to protect herself after being forced into this situation. While I didn't have any intentions of doing anything to her, I had four sisters that made me overly protective of all women when it came to their safety.

I rolled over, cringing when the bed creaked again beneath me. Finally, I gave up and moved to the couch. It was already ten times better than the bed, and within minutes, I was fast asleep.

The next morning, I was up first, so I went ahead and took a quick shower, not wanting to tie up the bathroom if she needed it. I dried off and was about to get dressed when I realized that I had left my clothes in the kitchen, on the counter. I had been so distracted making a pot of coffee that I hadn't paid attention before I jumped in the shower.

I wrapped the towel around my waist and opened the door, hoping to grab my clothes before Tiffany got up and saw me. I was looking over my shoulder, feeling relieved that the bedroom door was still closed, when I rounded the corner and ran right into her.

Her hands planted firmly against my chest as she let out a squeal. I lifted my hands defensively to keep from touching her while I was naked, but unfortunately, all of the movement had allowed the towel to loosen its grip around me and fell to the floor.

My hands darted down to cover myself as her eyes widened. Her mouth dropped open as she took a small step back and stared at my naked body in front of her as I scrambled to figure out a way to get my towel back on without showing her my dick.

"I'm sorry," I apologized, feeling the heat flush my cheeks.

"No, I'm sorry," she stuttered. "I didn't hear you coming."

Her face turned crimson as she covered her mouth.

"I mean, I didn't hear you walking down the hallway. Not that you were coming. Or not coming. I um—"

"It's fine," I said quickly, trying to stop this conversation before it got too out of control.

"I wasn't insinuating that you were--."

"Really, Tiffany, it's fine."

She took another step back and tried to keep her gaze from wandering, but I caught her anyway.

"I'm gonna go back to my room," she announced, pulling her shoulders back as she sucked in a deep breath.

I stood there, unable to move as she walked past me. I felt her eyes on me and glanced over my shoulder to find her checking out my naked ass.

Well, things just got awkward.

Five

Tiffany

"It was so huge that he couldn't fully cover it with *both* hands!" I whispered into the phone, covering the mouthpiece even though I was alone in my room.

"What did you do?" Charlie asked, almost squealing. She had been my best friend since we graduated high school.

"I didn't know what to do! I tried not to look, but it was hard."

"Oh, I'm sure it was," she cooed and then giggled.

"Not like that," I laughed, feeling the blush cover my skin again.

"Well, that's too bad. I'm sure that would have been a sight to see."

"If it's as nice as his ass, I bet it would be."

"You checked out his ass?"

"Yeah," I admitted, chewing my nail nervously. "But he turned around and caught me."

"He caught you!! Tiffany! You naughty girl." Her tone changed from shocked to approval within a matter of seconds.

"I don't even know how I'm going to look him in the eye now."

"Well, just imagine him naked," she suggested. "Oh, wait. You've already done that."

She laughed, bringing mine out with hers.

"It's not funny," I said as convincingly as possible. "I'm stuck with him for the next four days—maybe longer, while we're snowed in."

"I really don't see what the problem is. If it were me—I would already be taking advantage of that situation and hiding *all* of the towels in that damn cabin."

"You're so bad," I laughed.

"Yeah, but it would be a fun time. And seriously, Tiffany, with everything you've been through recently, you deserve to have some fun."

I felt the happiness quickly slip away. Part of escaping to a remote cabin in the middle of nowhere was to run away from the problems I left behind in Oregon. I wasn't ready to deal with them then, and I sure as hell wasn't ready to deal with them now.

"So, tell me about this place. What's it like?" she asked, changing the subject when I stayed silent for too long.

"It's so beautiful, Charlie. There's so much snow that I could spend all day curled up under a blanket, drinking coffee, and reading books and not have an ounce of regret."

"Are there a lot of cabins close to you, or is it as secluded as you hoped it would be?"

"Our cabin is at the very end of our row, so we get an unobstructed view of the woods and don't see any other cabins. There are a few rows of cabins, with probably ten or so in each row. There's a main lodge in the middle. It's all surrounded by thick forest."

"That sounds dreamy," she sighed. "We should go together next year."

"That would be nice," I agreed. "We'll probably have to book it early. It seems like they fill up fast."

"Well, we'll make sure we get ours. And I want a room with a dick."

"I think you mean deck," I corrected, laughing.

"You can have your deck, but I want a dick in mine. If you get one, I want one too."

"I didn't get one," I snorted. "It wasn't like it was planned or anything."

"Then I guess I wouldn't mess with fate too much. I mean, if she's lining it up for you that much, you should definitely *jump* on that opportunity."

"Well, on that note, I better get going," I said. "I'll talk to you soon."

We hung up, and I laid back on the bed, debating how long I could avoid seeing Luke. I grabbed my clothes from the bed and made sure I had a towel before I jumped in the shower and tried not to picture him in it not that long ago.

Six

Luke

I pressed the button to silence my mother's phone call as Tiffany came down the hall. She had showered and gotten ready, which gave us a little bit of time to avoid each other after the towel incident. I didn't know who was more embarrassed—her or me. I could honestly say that I had never seen that shade of red on a woman before, and I've been with my fair share of them.

I stuffed my phone into my pocket and tried to pose in a way that didn't look like I had been standing around waiting for her. She smiled when she saw me, nervously tucking a strand of hair behind her ear as she avoided looking me in the eyes.

"Did you want to head over to the dining hall and see what the breakfast options are?" I asked, fastening my watch on my wrist.

"Sure, that sounds great."

I grabbed my coat from the back of the chair, then handed her hers. We walked in silence, trying to keep our balance in the knee-deep snow before we reached the portion that had been cleared by the maintenance crew. Soon, we were inside where it was warm and free of dangerous hazards.

"Luke!"

I froze at the sound of my name, the shrill sound of her voice sending chills through my body. There was *no fucking way* that she was here right now. I swallowed hard, forcing down the nausea that was rising, and turned around stiffly.

Making her way toward me with the speed of a cheetah closing in on a gazelle, there was no way to run and pretend that I hadn't seen her. Her heels clicked annoyingly on the tile floor as she rushed over in her designer suit—oblivious to the weather outside.

"I've been trying to call you," she said, annoyed.

"I've been busy," I muttered, glancing at Tiffany, who was standing beside me, curious as to what was going on.

"I can see," she replied snidely as she looked Tiffany up and down, not bothering to hide the judgment on her face.

"What are you doing here, mom?" I asked, ready to get this over with.

"Well, when you *wouldn't* come home for Christmas, your father and I decided we would come to you. Laney found out that you were staying at this beautiful resort and knew that *this* was the place she wanted to have her wedding!" She pressed her hands together, her face squinched with excitement.

"I'm sure she'll enjoy hearing about it when you get back home. Now, if you'll excuse me, we were on our way to get some breakfast." I placed my hand on Tiffany's lower back and gently pushed to guide her away from my mother.

"Oh, there's no need for that." She waved her hand as if clearing away the absurd thought. "She's here with us. Well, technically, the whole family is. When she decided that she *had* to get married this weekend, everyone jumped at the opportunity to spend Christmas in this magical wonderland. We were so lucky to grab the last few rooms, I heard that they *overbooked,*" she whispered in disbelief.

I rolled my eyes and ran a hand down my face. She had to be kidding me. There was no way in hell that my entire family had all made it down here for a last-minute wedding for my bratty baby sister. Although that explained how they ended up short on rooms by the time I got here to check in.

"Sounds like Laney," I muttered.

"Oh, don't be grumpy, you ol' Grinch." She swatted at my chest playfully before turning her attention back to Tiffany. "And who are you, dear? My son seems to have lost his manners, not bothering to introduce me to his date."

Tiffany looked at me nervously, her mouth slightly open as she was about to speak, when someone from the lodge walked over and interrupted before she could.

"Mr. Lane, I apologize for interrupting, however, we needed to confirm whose credit card you wanted to keep on file for the cabin you're sharing."

I watched as my mom's eyes widened with surprise as she listened in, checking for Tiffany's reaction.

"Please use my card," I confirmed, holding my mom's gaze, willing her not to say anything and make a scene.

"Yes, sir. If there is anything we can do to make your stay more comfortable, please let us know. We hope you and Ms. Thompson enjoy your visit," her voice was pleasant yet heavy with forced sincerity.

She turned and walked away, leaving the air thick with tension.

"Well, now I see why you *couldn't* come home for Christmas," she scoffed.

Before I could say anything, my sister came rushing over, tears running down her face.

"Everything is falling apart," she cried, throwing herself into my mom's arms.

"Oh, honey, what happened?"

"I spoke with the manager and asked about having the wedding here on Christmas Eve. They said that they couldn't cater the reception with that short of notice because they didn't have anyone equipped to handle the large party. What am I supposed to do now?" Laney whined, not bothering to look up to see me standing there.

"Well then, I guess it's a good thing that your brother—the *wedding planner*—is here. Surely he'll know what to do."

My sister whipped around, rubbing her tears away with the back of her hand.

"Luke! Can you help me?"

"I don't know," I sighed, not wanting to be part of this drama but also feeling a little intrigued by the idea of proving to them once and for all that my job wasn't the joke they made it out to be. If I could pull this off and give my sister the wedding of her dreams on three days' notice—I would go down in the wedding planner hall of fame. Not that we had one—but I would be sure to start one.

"Please, Luke," she begged, standing as close to me as possible with her hands pressed together in prayer. She hadn't bothered to notice Tiffany yet because she was too focused on getting what she wanted.

I turned toward Tiffany, a devious smirk on my face.

"What do you say, baby? Do you think you're up for catering this wedding?"

She narrowed her eyes at me in confusion and searched for the answer to the question she didn't have to speak. I knew what she was thinking—*what in the hell is he doing!*

"Um, sure?" she replied with far too much uncertainty.

"Great! I'll talk to Julianna and get everything arranged," I said smugly to my mom and sister, my hand still pressed firmly against Tiffany's back. It wasn't necessary, given I had managed to shock her into a state of being paralyzed, but it made me feel better that I would at least feel the moment that she tried to run.

"Well, it looks like we'll finally get to see you in action as you put together your baby sister's *wedding of her dreams*."

I didn't miss the snide tone as my mother spoke. Thankfully, it just fueled the fire that was now raging inside me to prove that she didn't know me or what I was capable of.

"Laney, I'll need you to come by the cabin in an hour so we can discuss details. Don't be late. Your wedding is on the line."

She nodded but didn't say anything as she finally noticed Tiffany.

"Now, if you'll excuse us, we're heading to breakfast." I turned and guided her in the other direction, my hand gently sliding down her back and grazing her ass as my mom and sister watched. I didn't have to turn around to know that they had seen it because I could feel their eyes burning holes in the back of my head.

Once we were in the dining hall, Tiffany turned on me, shoving me up against a wall. Her emerald green eyes flashed with anger as her jaw tightened.

"What the hell was that?!" she demanded, making sure she kept her voice low enough not to draw attention to us.

"I'm sorry," I blew out, the adrenaline starting to wear off. "I didn't know what else to do. I panicked, and since my mom was already assuming that you are my girlfriend, I just went with it."

"You volunteered me to cater a wedding! I've never catered anything in my life! And then you throw a wedding at me with no warning whatsoever?"

"I know," I apologized, gently reaching out to hold her shoulders. "I should have asked you first and again, I'm sorry. I guess I just saw an opportunity, so I went for it."

"Because it made *you* look good. What happens when I mess everything up and ruin your sister's wedding?"

"You're not going to mess it up."

"How do you know that? You don't even know me."

"Fair enough," I shrugged. "I guess we'll have plenty of time getting to know each other over the next few days."

"This was supposed to be a *relaxing* week off," she muttered, her shoulders dropping.

"How about we make a deal?" I offered, pulling my hands away before it started to feel awkward.

She looked at me and waited, still looking as stressed as I was starting to feel.

"I'm starting to get a Pretty Woman vibe from this," she joked. "But, I'm listening."

"Well, for starters, if you do the catering for this wedding, I'll make sure that you're paid accordingly and that you are recognized as the caterer. Then after the wedding, I'll pay for you to stay in the cabin through New Years so you can soak in the giant tub and watch the snow fall. What do you say? Your first paid catering job and a week's stay paid for at this beautiful lodge?"

"I'll do the job," she sighed heavily. "But I'm not accepting your offer to stay another week at your expense. Thank you, but I can't do that."

"Why not?" It didn't make sense to me why she wouldn't want to stay another week and not have to pay for it.

"Because I'm not looking to take advantage of you or to have you spend your money on me. You're doing me a favor by getting me this job. I've been looking for a way to get my foot in the door, and now I have one."

I stared at her in disbelief. I had never met a woman who wasn't jumping at the opportunity to get something from me. Whether it be a girl that I was dating or my own family—someone always wanted something. Yet with Tiffany, all she wanted was a chance to do something on her own.

We went through the buffet and grabbed breakfast, neither of us bothering to say much as our minds raced with the details of what we needed to do to pull this wedding off. An hour later, we were back at our cabin, talking to Laney and Jake about the extravagant wedding that she insisted on having.

Seven

Tiffany

My head felt like it was going to explode from the enormous amount of information that had been shoved into it since this morning. I kind of missed when my only problem was looking Luke in the eye after seeing him naked. Now, I was responsible for catering his sister's *small* wedding of a hundred and fifty people.

My palms had been sweating all day as my nerves ran wild. I tried to remind myself that I didn't have to worry about the small details of what Laney wanted because that was Luke's job. So what if she wanted hibiscus flowers lining the walkway to the altar or demanded that they have a live band perform at the reception. I snorted when she insisted that she wanted to have one dozen doves released when they said "I do," earning a dirty look from her.

We were on our way to meet with Julianna, and even I was

impressed with how well Luke did his job as a wedding planner. The confident and direct man I had heard on the phone yesterday was in full charge today. We walked to the main hall and waited at the front desk as the receptionist called to let her know we were there. A few minutes later, we were led down a long hall to a large office with a beautiful view of the snow-capped mountains.

"Luke," she said evenly, shaking his hand when we walked in. "I wasn't expecting to work with you again before the end of the year."

"Yeah, I wasn't expecting it either," he laughed. "But my baby sister threw me one hell of a curveball, so here we are."

"Well, I'm happy to help however I can."

Luke introduced me before we all sat down, and I pulled out the notepad and pen that I had swiped from the room before we left. I had no idea what notes I would take, but I wanted to feel prepared.

"As I've told your sister, we simply don't have the staff to cater the wedding," Julianna said, leaning back in the tall leather chair. She looked to be close to his age with soft wrinkles around her amber eyes. Her features were soft, but she carried her attitude well. I couldn't imagine that she got to the position she was in as the executive director of the lodge by letting anyone walk all over her.

"Yes, she's told me. However, I have a solution to your problem," Luke said, grinning at me before looking back to Julianna. "Tiffany can cater the wedding. If you can provide the ingredients, the kitchen and waitstaff, then she can handle organizing and running the kitchen to make sure everything runs smoothly."

She turned in her chair and studied me for a moment.

"What events have you catered in the past?"

"None," I admitted nervously.

"She has the experience that you need," Luke assured her.

She pursed her lips as she thought about it.

"If you want this wedding to happen here, you need her a lot more than she needs you," he added.

"Fine. But I'll need to check references," she said dryly. She picked up her pen and pulled a notepad over to write on. "What culinary references do you have?"

"I've only had one, but I would rather that you don't call them."

I knew that this would be what kept her from hiring me and chewed the inside of my cheek.

"Why not?"

"Because," I looked sheepishly at Luke, who was waiting for an explanation as well. "I didn't leave on good terms."

I swallowed down the panic that was threatening to rise.

She didn't say anything, just looked at Luke and raised an eyebrow that confirmed her *you've got to be kidding me* look that was plastered across her face.

"What happened?" Luke asked softly, ignoring Julianna.

I sucked in a deep breath and lowered my head. My hands trembled in my lap as I fought to find the courage to speak. Charlie was the only person I had told what happened, and she was still begging me to let her handle things for me.

"I was promised a position as an executive chef, however, I didn't find out until it was too late that the owner wanted something in exchange for that title. When I refused to sleep with him, he fired me and tried to force himself on me anyway."

My leg shook as my emotions flooded through me.

"What did you do?" Julianna asked, setting her pen on the desk and leaning back casually in her chair.

"I kneed him in the balls and left. Then, when he tried to reach for me again, I grabbed the cast iron skillet from the counter and hit him with it. It knocked him out long enough for me to get away."

"Wow," Luke said quietly, reaching over to rest his hand on my knee. "I'm so sorry that you had to go through that."

"Thank you," I let out the breath that I had been holding. "It's still pretty fresh, and I honestly don't know what I'm going to do when I go home. I have a chance to start over, but I don't know where to begin."

"Any woman who can handle a jerk like that can sure as hell handle the men in my kitchen. The catering job is yours," she said with a smile. "And I'm trusting Luke's recommendation that you're qualified to handle the position."

"Thank you," I replied, trying to contain my excitement.

"I'll take you to the kitchen so you can meet the staff and start working on the planning and preparations. Do you have a menu in mind that you wanted to make? We may or may not have the supplies you need, so you might have to get creative."

"Um, well, no," I laughed nervously. "I haven't had time to think about a menu, but I can put one together rather quickly once I know what my options are."

"Perfect," Julianna said, standing up. "There will be a food tasting tomorrow afternoon, so please make sure you have everything you need before then. If the food is approved at the tasting, then you can proceed with setting everything up for the wedding."

"And if you don't approve?" I asked, knowing that I would regret it.

"Then the bride will be rather disappointed that her guests will be visiting our buffet that night with the rest of the guests."

I felt the air whoosh through me as my head started spinning. There was no pressure *whatsoever.*

Eight

Luke

I stood back and watched Tiffany take control of the kitchen as if she naturally belonged there. Julianna had been kind enough to do the introduction, but after that, Tiffany wasted no time setting the tone with the kitchen and waitstaff. She talked with the executive chef and discussed menu options, before checking out the inventory.

"That's all there is?" she asked, panicked, as she came out of the walk-in freezer.

"Unfortunately, yes. Our next shipment of meat won't be in until after the wedding."

"Okay," she exhaled, tapping her fingers together as her beautiful mind worked. "Since the steaks are thick, let's cut them into smaller portions, and that will double what we have. We can also add a vegetarian dish to save on meat, and I'm thinking we can have pizza for the kids. We'll use half of the salmon, half of the chicken, and three-quarters of the steak for the wedding, while the rest of it can be used for the buffet."

"That can work," he agreed, making a note on the worn-out paper in his hand. "We already have the Christmas day meal planned with the ham and turkey, so we don't have to worry about meat that day. We'll get our new shipment the next morning."

"Perfect. I think that will handle the food. I'll put together the menu, and then we can sit down again and make sure we have everything that we'll need."

She finished writing her notes and looked around to find me. I pushed off of the wall and walked over to where she was standing as the kitchen started to fill with noise while the staff got back to work.

"How'd it go?" I asked, even though I knew because I had been standing there the whole time.

"Good. I think we might be able to pull this off after all," she laughed, walking with me toward the door. "I just need to figure out *what* to cook and then hope that Julianna likes it when I make it for her tomorrow."

"Um, about that," I said nervously, pulling out my phone to show her the email that had just come through. "It won't be just her."

"What are you talking about?" she asked, leaning forward to read the email. A few seconds later, her head whipped up as she pinned me with a look.

"I'm cooking dinner for your family tomorrow, as well as the upper management of the lodge?"

"Yeah," I said slowly, worried that she was about to find a cast-iron skillet and whop me with it like she did that dirtbag at her last job.

"How many people?" she asked with her eyes closed and shoulders tense.

"Twenty-five."

She opened her eyes and glared at me.

"Fine. But you're going to pay for this," she teased.

I chewed my bottom lip, figuring now was as good of a time as any to add the other bad news.

"Also, my mom already told everyone that we're dating, so they're going to expect us to be *together* tomorrow night."

"What is that supposed to mean?"

"It means that I need you to pretend to be my girlfriend for the next few days, at least until my family leaves after the wedding."

She rubbed her lips together while shaking her head and resting her hand on her hip.

"You owe me big."

Nine

Tiffany

"I've put together a delectable menu that is sure to please all of your guests," I said nervously as I stood in front of the two round tables in the ballroom where the wedding would take place in two days. I could feel everyone's attention on me as I tried not to pass out.

"The first item," I said as my voice caught in my throat. "Is a steak au poivre, with a side of roasted red potatoes and served with a creamy cognac-based sauce. The second item is chicken francese, which is a pan-fried chicken breast with a buttery lemon sauce, served with a side of savory mashed potatoes. Next is a honey garlic glazed salmon with a side of white rice. All entrees are accompanied by a spinach strawberry salad with a poppy seed dressing. For the children's menu, I've prepared a pepperoni pizza and side salad."

I pulled in a long, steady, deep breath to replace the oxygen that I had just expended getting all of that information out as quickly as possible. Ernesto, the executive chef, had helped me prepare the meal, and the waitstaff had assisted with serving the equally portioned plates that had a small sample of each item I'd mentioned. I hated using potatoes for the side on two dishes, but given the limited ingredients available, there weren't many choices.

"Thank you, Tiffany," Julianna said. "Everything looks and smells wonderful, I can't wait to try what you've prepared for us."

I smiled nervously before sitting down next to Luke, ready for the attention to be off of me. The room started to fill with noise as everyone began eating and talking about the different flavors. So far, the feedback sounded positive, but then again, I could only hear the people around us at our table, which included the upper management. Even if they didn't like it, they were trained to be professional enough not to say so in front of everyone else.

"You did great," Luke whispered as he leaned in close to me.

"Thank you, I was so nervous that I don't know if I even said the right words."

He looked around at the heads that were all hung as they focused on their food.

"I don't see a single person complaining," he laughed. "Now start eating before your food gets cold. It would be a shame to miss the best meal you've had since you've been here."

I giggled, knowing that it was true, and cut into my thin strip of steak. I had to portion everything perfectly to make sure there was enough meat for this meal, as well as for what I needed for the wedding. Ernesto and I agreed to use three of the steaks that were supposed to go to the buffet for today instead and cut them thin enough that we could serve twenty-six people, including myself.

We ate in silence, my stomach thankful for the food, given that I had been too nervous to eat this morning.

When everyone was done, the waitstaff came by to collect our plates before serving coffee and refilling the glasses of water. The tables had turned, and now it was the local baker who was up to present the cake options. I was thankful for the shift in attention but still felt uneasy that they would come back and say that the bride and groom weren't impressed with my food.

I leaned back in my seat and listened as the short, curvy woman in a *You're Baking Me Crazy* apron explained the layers of the cake and the filling options. I felt eyes on me and slowly looked around the room, finding Luke's mom staring at us and not paying any attention to the speaker.

"Your mom is watching us," I whispered without moving my mouth, trying to be as discreet as possible.

Luke didn't say anything, but I noticed how his head slightly turned to the side to confirm. Next, his arm came up and wrapped around my shoulders, resting on the back of the chair. It was meant to make her see that we were a couple, but it was odd that it didn't feel weird to me. I didn't fight the feeling of him suddenly being too close. Instead, I craved it.

I shifted in my seat, resting my back against his side as I reached up and laced my fingers with his. If he wanted to put on a show for his family, I was happy to help him do it. I knew she was still watching when I tilted my head back and whispered something in his ear, letting my breath tickle the stubble that dotted his jawline.

While his mom probably imagined that I was saying dirty things to him, I had really just informed him that there was a sale at the pet store and that I was going to beat him at Mall Madness again when we got back to our cabin.

I felt the vibrations of his chuckle as his chest rumbled with it. He leaned closer and playfully nipped my earlobe before threatening me with a game of Monopoly instead. It was the most basic conversation, but we made it seem like we were two people who were madly in love and couldn't keep our hands off of each other.

Once the baker was finished, we were served samples of cake. I slid a small piece onto my fork and then turned to Luke, licking my lips as I offered him the bite. He slowly wrapped his mouth around the fork, locking eyes with me as his hand reached up and gently held mine. He took the bite and then stole my fork, offering me another one.

We sat there, flirting shamelessly with each other while his mother continued to watch us. Everything was almost wrapped up, and I was ready to get out of there and outside where the cold air could lift this fog I was in. As we were heading out, I heard footsteps quickly approaching behind us. My stomach knotted, knowing that his mom was probably tracking us down to give a lecture about inappropriate behavior. He had already warned me to expect it.

Instead, Julianna called out my name, and we stopped. Her face was lit up with a smile that spread across it.

"You got the job!" she squealed excitedly, pulling me in for a hug. "Everyone *loved* your food and are still talking about it!"

"What?!" I gasped in disbelief. "That's amazing!"

"I won't keep you guys, I just wanted to share the exciting news! Have a wonderful night celebrating, and I'll see you in a few days at the wedding."

She smiled and rushed off to the sound of someone calling her name. I turned to look at Luke, a goofy smile on my face, still not believing it myself.

"Congratulations," he said, his lips turned up in the corners. "I knew you could do it."

He leaned forward and gently grabbed the sides of my face before planting his lips on mine. Everything felt perfect about it, but this time, no one else was watching.

Ten

Luke

I couldn't believe that I had kissed her, but when she kissed me back, I knew that I couldn't stop. Once we got back to the cabin, our hands desperately rushed to get clothes off while our mouths devoured each other.

"Are you sure you want to do this?" I asked between kisses as she pulled her sweater over her head and flung it across the room.

"Yes," she panted before wrapping her arms around my neck and kissing me. She was down to just her bra and panties, and I was desperate to see her. My chest heaved as I tried to catch my breath, breaking from the kiss for a second to open the door to the bedroom. I hadn't asked her whether she wanted to go in there, but when she led me down the hallway, I assumed that's where she wanted to take this.

I walked her to the bed, hearing her giggle as she bumped into it before I gently pushed her down on it. I took a moment to look at her beautiful body as she laid on the bed, her blond hair fanned out around her. I knew that her body was curvy and that she was self-conscious about it, but seeing her lay on the bed wearing nothing but her bra and panties, she looked sexy as hell. Her chest moved quickly as her breathing increased with anticipation, making her plump breasts dance on display.

I grabbed a condom from my wallet then tossed my jeans to the floor before stripping off my underwear. She locked eyes with me, reluctant to look down at my cock as it grew thicker by the second. I took my time stroking it while watching the way her breathing changed the more turned on she got. When she looked like she couldn't take it anymore, I took the last few steps to the bed and crawled on top of her, holding myself up on my elbow.

Slowly, I kissed her neck while my free hand caressed her breast through the thin fabric of her bra. I could feel her nipple harden beneath my touch and longed to suck it. I made my way down her neck before reaching behind her and unclasping her bra. Once it was undone, I worked the straps down her arms and flung it across the room.

She smiled and pulled her bottom lip between her teeth

when she saw the hungry look on my face. I leaned down and began kissing her breasts, teasing her before I pulled a nipple into my mouth and sucked. She moaned and muttered a string of curse words before digging her fingers into my hair and pressing my head tighter against her.

My dick was throbbing with the need to be inside of her. I kept my mouth focused on sucking her nipples while my hand slid down her stomach and over her pussy. I dipped a finger inside her slit, feeling how wet she was already. She parted her legs, allowing me more access as I pushed another finger in and started fingering her.

She felt so good wrapped around my fingers that I couldn't wait to feel her around my cock. I wanted to make sure that she was ready before that happened, so I took the time to move down her body and teased her clit with my tongue. She moaned even louder this time as her knees fell open. I looked up to find her head back and eyes closed as she caressed her breasts, flicking her thumb over her nipples.

If I kept watching what she was doing to herself, I was going to come before I was even inside of her. I sucked harder as my fingers fucked her fast, drawing her orgasm out of her as she clenched and spasmed around me. I couldn't take it any longer. Once she was finished, I rolled onto my back and rushed to get the condom on.

She was smiling sexily at me as she waited, propping herself up on her elbows as she watched me cover myself. Her eyes shamelessly traveled down to my throbbing cock and took it in. She licked her lips before looking up at me, the desire flashing in her eyes. She laid back down on the bed and spread her legs, waiting for me to slide inside of her.

I got up and stood at the edge of the bed, pulling her hips toward me until her ass was hanging halfway off the bed but supported by my thighs. I loved the perfectly unobstructed view of her wet pussy, knowing that I was the reason she was practically dripping. I kept my eyes locked on hers as I grabbed my cock and guided it inside of her.

My eyes closed as she gasped, her pussy eagerly clenching around me. It was our first time together, and I didn't want to look like some fifteen-year-old boy who couldn't control himself. I grabbed her legs and pushed them together, making sure I was still snug inside of her. Resting them against my chest, I wrapped my arm around them to make sure she stayed in place before I started thrusting. The sound of our bodies slapping against each other was overly stimulating, bringing me closer to the edge as my balls felt the sting of hitting her ass with each hard movement.

"Oh God, yes," she moaned, her hands roaming over her breasts again. "Fuck me harder," she begged.

I did as she asked, pumping as hard as I could while quickening my pace. The harder I fucked her, the louder her moans became. The way she moaned my name had me wishing I could listen to it forever.

Her hand slipped down and started rubbing her clit, and I could feel the way her body was reacting. I looked down and watched as she let her legs fall open to the sides, giving me the perfect view again. My dick looked huge as it pushed through her swollen pink lips that were glistening wet. Her fingers desperately rubbed her clit in circles while her other hand worked her nipples.

Even if she hadn't groaned loudly, I would have still known that she was coming again from how tight her pussy was wrapped around my dick. I felt my orgasm rip through me as I gave her a few more fast, hard pumps as I spilled my load into the condom.

We were both breathless and sweaty as I pulled out of her.

"You're so fucking beautiful," I whispered, leaning down to kiss her.

Eleven

Tiffany

My body was pleasantly sore from the multiple orgasms and the best sex I had ever had. Hands down—the best EVER. I didn't bother getting up from the bed while he went and cleaned up. There was no energy for that. I was totally and completely spent.

A few minutes later, he came back into the room and looked unsure whether he should get dressed or what he should do.

"Come lay with me," I offered, scooting over and patting the bed beside me.

"You sure?" he asked, his voice softer than usual.

I nodded and closed my eyes, hoping that I didn't fall asleep.

The bed dipped as he climbed up next to me and laid down.

I rolled onto my side and laid my hand on his chest, trailing small circles through his hair.

He moved closer so I could lay my head on his shoulder as he wrapped his arm under my neck.

"How are you feeling?" he asked, gently rubbing my back.

"Wonderful," I sighed. "That was amazing."

He chuckled and kissed the top of my head.

"What about you?"

"Same."

His answer was short and simple, yet I believed him based on how relaxed his body was next to me.

I didn't know what all of this meant, but for once, I wasn't concerned with trying to figure it out. We laid together, our breathing falling in sync as we drifted asleep on the bed.

At some point in the middle of the night, he must have gotten cold because I woke up to find him still in bed beside me, with a blanket from the living room wrapped around us. I looked at the window and saw that the sun was already up, which meant that we needed to get the day going.

The wedding was tomorrow which meant that there was still a ton left for us to do today, and I likely wouldn't see him most of the day. I would be in the kitchen with Ernesto, preparing the food for tomorrow, as well as for the rehearsal dinner tonight, while Luke would be meeting with everyone else and running at full speed.

I rolled over and gently kissed his lips, hoping it would be a good way to wake him up. He kept his eyes closed as his hand reached behind my head and pulled me closer as he started kissing my neck again. I was close enough to feel the heat coming off of his body and knew not to look beneath the blanket. He was hard and already ready for more.

"We have to get ready, or you're gonna be late this morning," I warned.

"I can be quick," he murmured, his hand roaming down to my breast.

"Alright, Romeo," I laughed and pulled away. "But at least multi-task."

I got up and walked off, winking over my shoulder as he watched me shake my ass for him before making it to the hallway. I went to the bathroom and turned on the shower, giving it a few minutes to warm up while brushing my teeth.

A few minutes later, he joined me with a condom in one hand and his hard dick in the other. We climbed in the shower and wasted no time cleaning each other's bodies before he turned me around and took me from behind as the water rained down my back.

Once we were finished getting ready, we grabbed a quick breakfast in the dining hall before heading our separate ways while I tried to force myself not to think about what had happened between us. I had a job to do and needed to focus on that instead.

I had spent the morning with Ernesto preparing the food for the rehearsal dinner. Thankfully, the groom was more laid back than the bride and had asked for pub food instead of a fancy seated meal. It was the only item that she had compromised on, but I was happy to have a lighter menu of hot wings and mini sliders to prepare instead of two big meals with several dishes. Tonight's dinner would be served buffet style, which meant that I wouldn't be needed after the food was served. I would have time to spend with Luke *if* he wanted to. As far as I knew, we were still supposed to be pretending to date, so I couldn't imagine that I wouldn't attend the rehearsal dinner with him as his date.

Around one o'clock, Ernesto took a lunch break and offered to bring me food on his way back. I declined and worked

"What are you doing?" she giggled, reaching down to make sure her dress was covering her butt.

"Making sure your shoes don't get wet, and you don't lose a toe to frostbite."

"I'll be fine," she laughed. The sound of it felt wonderful against my chest.

"Okay, so maybe I just wanted to hold you before we got there, and I had to keep my hands off of you."

"Is that why your hand keeps grabbing my ass?"

"Nope, not at all. That's for your safety, to make sure that you're secure and not going to fall."

"Mmhmm."

I laughed, feeling the joy radiating through me. I wanted the moment to last as long as possible before we got into the ballroom, and it was ruined by my family.

A few minutes later, we were heading toward the entrance and had reached dry land. I carefully set her down, making sure she was steady before letting go of her. I reached down to hold her hand when I remembered her injury. It was bandaged nicely with plenty of gauze, but I still wondered whether she needed stitches after all when I saw that it had been bleeding again.

on cutting the meat for the wedding so we could get that out of the way. I was deep in the zone and hadn't heard anyone walk up behind me when a voice startled me, and the knife I was using went straight through my thumb.

"Son of a bitch!" I yelled, dropping the knife into the sink and moving my hand away from the food as quickly as possible. Red spots splattered the sink as I looked around for something to use to stop the bleeding.

"Oh, dear!" Luke's mom exclaimed, rushing beside me with a clean towel from the counter behind me. "Here, let me see your hand," she demanded, holding her hand out for me.

I eyed her carefully, not sure why she was back here to begin with. I lifted my hand and laid it on the towel, frowning when the blood-soaked it immediately. She wrapped it tightly and put pressure on the cut.

"There, there," she said quietly. "Let's see if we can stop the bleeding. Try to be still and don't move."

I did as she said, still feeling guarded as to why she was here.

"What are you doing back here?" I asked, keeping my tone level.

"Well, I came to talk to you about the menu. The nice young man at the hostess station said I could find you back here. I didn't mean to startle you, though."

"I wasn't expecting anyone," I admitted.

"I can see that," she laughed lightly, gently lifting the towel to check the bleeding. Her brows pulled together when she noticed the bleeding hadn't slowed down yet. Without losing the pressure that she already had on it, she carefully reached behind her and grabbed another towel, wrapping it around the one that was currently soaked with my blood.

I felt my stomach tighten when I wondered why she wanted to talk about the menu. If she was going to demand some last-minute change—I would lose my shit. Everything was falling together nicely, but it was a very delicate balance to keep it that way.

"So, what did you want to talk about?" I asked, ready to just get it over with.

"Well, I just wanted to tell you how much I enjoyed the meal that you prepared last night." She kept her eyes on my hand as she spoke, not bothering to look up. "You and Luke seem to be quite the team."

And there it was.

"He's easy to work with and has done a wonderful job putting this wedding together on such short notice."

"Yes, we're all thankful for that," she said with a hint of sarcasm in her voice that got under my skin. "Just as I'm sure you're thankful for him getting you this job. I think we can all safely say that you haven't been dating long, so I had to wonder what was in it for you."

She studied me closely, trying to gauge my reaction. I kept my face straight as I pulled my hand away from her and held it close to my chest. I had no idea whether the bleeding had stopped or not, but I didn't want her touching me.

"I'm thankful for everything that Luke does for me," I said sharply, hearing someone approaching. "Like the multiple orgasms he gave me last night and the quickie we had in the shower this morning."

Her jaw dropped open just in time for Luke to walk around the corner. His face confirmed that he heard everything.

She clutched her chest in fake surprise, acting as if I had just told her that he had eight eyes and a cock made of titanium.

"Mother," Luke said coldly, coming to stand beside me. "What are you doing here?"

He looked down at the bloody towel wrapped around my hand and glanced at me, concerned.

"I was just coming to tell Tiffany how much I enjoyed her food last night."

"And to question how I got this job," I bit out sharply.

"She got the job because she's qualified for it. It shows in her food that *you* had no problem devouring last night. And just for the record—it's none of your business how she got the job."

"Oh, please," she muttered. "We all know that this isn't a real relationship, Luke. You can stop pretending and let your sister have the attention she deserves for her wedding."

He turned his back to her and gently reached for my hand, shaking his head while he ignored her comment.

"What happened?"

"I didn't hear her coming and accidentally cut myself."

"Can I see?"

I nodded, sucking in a deep breath as he slowly pulled the towel away. Thankfully the bleeding had stopped for the most part.

"Do you need to have this looked at?" he asked, turning his head to get a better look.

"I think it'll be fine," I assured him. "It's stopped bleeding, so I shouldn't need stitches. I can ask Ernesto to help with the cutting work while I focus on the other prep."

"Okay, if you need anything, just let me know."

"Thank you."

For a moment, it felt like it was just the two of us until his mom cleared her throat to remind us that she was still there.

"I just stopped by to say hi, but I've gotta get going. I'm meeting with the photographer and the DJ here in a few minutes."

"Okay," I smiled. "Thanks for stopping by, that was a nice surprise."

"I'll see you at the rehearsal dinner." His smile brightened as he said it.

"You're seriously bringing her to your sister's rehearsal dinner?" his mom scoffed.

I watched the anger flash through his eyes before he turned and glared at her.

"Why wouldn't I?"

"I just thought you would have more respect for your family than to bring some floozie that you barely know to your sister's wedding. Like I said, we're all onto your game, and you're not fooling anyone. If you need to try to prove to us that you're not gay, then fine, so be it. But I thought you had more class than this." She tossed a nod in my direction.

I felt the sting of her words as I flinched away from them.

Luke reached down and wrapped a hand around my waist, pulling me closer to him.

"The only one who's been putting on a show is you. If you have a problem with Tiffany being there as my girlfriend, then I'll make it easy for everyone, and *neither* of us will be there. Just be sure to remember who it was that pulled this shit show of a wedding off when *you* couldn't."

She narrowed her eyes at him before turning and storming out of the room.

Once the coast was clear, I turned to him and smiled sadly.

"I'm sorry, I didn't mean to cause problems for you with your family."

"You didn't," he said calmly. "For the first time in a long

time, you've helped me to see things clearly when it comes to family."

"How's that?"

"I've always thought that I didn't want to fall in love—I purposely avoided it at all costs. But being with you these past few days has shown me a different view of love and what it could be. You're nothing like my mom and sisters. You don't demand things or expect that everything goes your way. You're funny, and genuine, and caring. You're everything that they're not, and it opened my eyes to what I want in life."

"And what's that?" I asked, reaching up and wrapping my arm around his neck as I searched for the golden flecks in his eyes that I had come to love.

"I want to be snowed in with no place to go while losing to you at Mall Madness and making love to you all night long. I don't care about anything else—I want those moments with you because they make me feel like I'm finally happy, and I look forward to when I get to see you again."

"I feel the same way," I said nervously. "But is it too soon for us to feel this way about each other?"

"I don't think so," he shook his head, gently caressing

my cheek with his knuckles. "I think that when you have someone who makes you happy without even trying, that's something worth holding onto. We have a chemistry that's stronger than I've ever felt with anyone else, and that tells me that there's something there. Something that makes me want to do whatever I can to make you happy so I can see that beautiful smile that lights up your entire face."

I felt butterflies in my stomach as his words hit me straight in the heart.

"I really do need to get going," he said, slowly pulling away. "But I'll come pick you up around 6 for the rehearsal dinner if that works for you?"

"Sure, that sounds nice." I smiled, fighting the urge to protest and tell him that I shouldn't go. If *he* wanted me to go with him, then I was going to. His mother was rude and borderline intimidating, but that wasn't going to keep me away from him. Besides, we had already come this far with proving that we were in a relationship, I wasn't going to stop now and give her the satisfaction of knowing that she was right. He deserved better than that.

He turned and left, leaving me with a warm fuzzy feeling that I hoped didn't go away any time soon.

Twelve

Luke

It was 5:45, and I had confirmed that the rehearsal dinner was good to go and that the buffet would be opened promptly at 6:15. Ernesto and his team had taken over with plenty of direction from Tiffany. This meant that the kitchen and waitstaff would handle everything, and Tiffany would be free for the rest of the evening.

I walked back to the cabin and smiled when I found Tiffany inside wearing a pleated black dress that hit just above her knee. Her hair was pinned up nicely on top of her head with a few strands that hung around her face in delicate, soft curls that complimented the light makeup she was wearing. The neckline was flattering and high enough not to expose any cleavage, but the rose gold pendant that hung from the thin chain around her neck dipped right at the top, reminding me of her beautiful breasts that I couldn't wait to get my hands on again.

"Are you ready?" she asked, pulling her black peacoat on and smoothing down the front of her dress.

"You look incredible," I said, unable to think straight. "You're so beautiful."

"Thank you." She smiled and tucked a curl behind her ear. "I couldn't decide what to wear. Everything else was too casual, and I didn't want to stick out like a sore thumb more than I already do. This was the only dress that I brought with me."

"It's perfect. Although I will admit one thing," I teased. "You look so good that I'm thinking that we should skip the rehearsal dinner and stay here instead."

"You're so bad," she teased, smacking my chest lightly with the clutch in her hand. "Let's go before we're late."

I followed her out of the door, taking the opportunity to check out her ass in the dress and the way her heels made her legs look longer.

The snow had started to fall again, making it hard for her to walk through it without soaking her feet. I watched as she studied the area around her and tried to figure out the best path to take. Instead, I reached over and picked her up, carrying her in my arms.

I was so focused on her hand that I hadn't noticed anyone heading our way, until I heard my name.

"Luke!" Laney shrieked, rushing over with her arms extended. She ran into my arms and wrapped me in a hug. "Everything is perfect and beautiful, thank you so much!"

"You deserve the best," I said, planting a quick kiss on the top of her head.

"I appreciate all of it," she replied, pulling back. She looked at Tiffany and smiled. "And thank you for helping with the catering. My brother told me everything you've done for us, and it means so much to me. You're an amazing chef!"

"Thank you," Tiffany said, her cheeks blushing at the compliment. "It's been my pleasure."

"Well, I'm going to go grab my phone before dinner starts. I'll see you guys in there," Laney said, smiling as she rushed off and left us behind.

"Are you ready to do this?" I asked, noticing how nervous Tiffany seemed.

"Yes. Let's go practice eating dinner," she joked, laughing nervously.

I placed my hand on her lower back and led her into the

room that was already filled with the majority of my family and some of Laney's friends. I didn't have to scan the tables to know where we were sitting since I was the one who had organized everything. Much to my mother's dismay, I had seated Tiffany and myself at another table, away from her and my sisters. When asked about why I had done it, I pretended that there wasn't enough room for us to all sit together, so obviously, we should sit at another table to make room for everyone.

I walked her over to our seats and held her chair out for her. Julianna was already seated next to Tiffany and smiled when we joined her and the few other staff members. It made sense that we would sit at this table, given that I was now the *hired* wedding planner and Tiffany was the caterer. My mom liked to make a big show of how much money they spent on things, and I made sure she had plenty to brag about with how much this wedding was going to cost my parents. I didn't go overboard but made sure that Tiffany received a fifteen percent bonus for the last-minute job.

"Luke, everything looks wonderful," Julianna cooed. "I think you've outdone yourself."

"Thank you," I said coolly, adjusting my tie and unbuttoning my jacket as I sat down. "In all fairness, we've only done a few weddings here, and they were in the summer at the stables."

"Well, I think we've got a new venue to look at for your winter weddings if you're interested. Maybe a new caterer too?"

"We'll discuss options after this one is over. Let's make sure everything goes off without a hitch first," I chuckled.

I spotted my mom from across the room, glowering at us and making no effort to hide the disgusted look on her face. I smiled smugly and lifted my glass of wine in the air to her, raising my eyebrows. That pissed her off even more as she grabbed my aunt Jolene by the arm and rushed her off to the side to talk about me.

I took a sip, allowing the merlot to calm some of the nerves I was starting to feel. Tiffany and Julianna talked about the plans for tomorrow and discussed options for getting someone else to help when she noticed Tiffany's hand. I was impressed with how well she handled herself, and not once had I seen her look intimated or unsure of herself after being thrown into the middle of all of this. She handled everything with grace and looked like a total pro, which made me proud to have her on my arm tonight as my date, as well as the incredible chef that everyone was starting to rave about again as they got their food.

We ate and talked, enjoying the company of those around us. It felt nice to have genuine conversation without feeling constantly judged. Tiffany was a hit and had everyone's attention as she tossed her head back, laughing, telling a story about a time when she accidentally caught her sleeve on fire and set off the sprinklers in the kitchen at work. Her mother— who was almost as bad as mine—didn't bother asking if she was okay after suffering a burn. Instead, she lectured her about not getting the hot firefighter's phone number.

Once we were finished, we made our way around the room, saying hello to my family and mingling for a few minutes, before it was deemed an appropriate amount of time to excuse ourselves without being rude. I could care less about visiting with everyone, I just wanted to get back to the cabin and have some alone time with Tiffany.

We were wrapping up when I turned to head out the door. My jaw dropped when I saw who had just walked in. Tiffany was completely oblivious to the drama that was about to unfold right in front of her.

"Hey there, handsome," she said seductively, running a freshly manicured fingernail down the length of my tie. I reached out and grabbed her wrist before she got any lower, our hands hovering over my belt buckle. "Such a tease," she winked.

"What are you doing here?" I asked, my voice low and angry.

"Laney invited me."

"She shouldn't have."

"Aww, is that really how you want to treat me?" She stuck out her bottom lip and fake pouted. Her raven black hair was pulled back into a slick ponytail that swished down her bare back from the dress that dipped down so far it barely covered her ass. The front didn't cover much more than the back with a plunging neckline that barely contained her breasts. I looked at her and then at Tiffany, noticing the apparent differences between them.

Tiffany looked between us, an awkward smile on her face as she tried to figure out what was going on.

"This is June," I said tightly, shoving my hands into my pockets. The soft silk of the fabric reminded me that we were in a public place where I couldn't make a scene.

"Oh, are you Luke's family?" Tiffany asked innocently.

"No," June hissed, eyeing Tiffany callously. "I'm his wife."

Thirteen

Tiffany

"I don't want to hear it!" I screamed, slamming the bedroom door behind me. My feet were frozen after I took off my heels to trek through the snow without falling. I was too angry to be anywhere near Luke and didn't want his family to see us fighting. I held out as long as possible, plastering the smile on my face as I met *his wife.*

His WIFE. How the hell did he not tell me that he was married? After our conversation earlier about finding that special someone that makes you happy and not having to work hard at a relationship that comes so easily--- well, apparently that was a bunch of bullshit.

I stepped out of the dress, laying it on the bed as I grabbed my sweats and put them on. I couldn't tell if I was shivering because I was still cold or if it was because I was so livid with him. I had finally given in and let my walls down long enough to let him in, and it bit me in the ass. How had I been so stupid to believe his lies? I blamed it on reading too many romance novels. It was the perfect setting for a book—stranded in a winter wonderland with an attractive stranger who just happens to be your soulmate while surrounded by the freshly fallen snow and some Christmas magic. There's always some sort of Christmas magic in those books.

But the problem was that this wasn't a book. It was my life, and it was going to hell in a handbag faster than a sinking ship. I pulled my phone out of my clutch and dialed Charlie's number, desperate to talk to her. I glanced at the time, not sure if it was too late, then remembered that she was usually up at all hours of the night anyway, doing things I only dreamed of.

"Hey," she said breathlessly. "What's up?"

"Are you doing what I think you're doing?" I asked, feeling slightly annoyed that she was having sex while I was in the middle of a meltdown—not that she knew I was.

"No," she laughed. "I just got home from the grocery store, and I didn't want to make two trips, so I lugged all of the bags upstairs at once, and now I'm out of breath."

I rolled my eyes and felt the smile tugging at my lips. It was good to talk to her, and she was already starting to calm my nerves some.

"So, what's up? Aren't you supposed to be at the rehearsal dinner tonight then having more hot sex?" she asked.

"Yeah, well, that's over," I huffed.

"Why? What happened?"

"He's married."

I heard her gasp and waited.

"Like *married* married?"

"Like I just met his wife fifteen minutes ago married."

"I don't understand. I thought you said that he was single?"

"Yeah, I thought he was too. He never mentioned anything about a wife. I guess it's my fault for not asking before we had sex."

I sighed and reached up to pull the bobby pins out of my hair. I was already starting to get a headache and didn't need the tension in my head to make it worse.

"Ugh," I groaned. "Everything happened *so fast*. Why didn't you talk me out of this when I first told you?"

I knew it wasn't her fault, but it made me feel better to think that someone else shared some of the blame in this.

"You mean when you were drooling over his monstrous one-eyed beast?" She laughed harder, and I found myself getting the giggles.

"Okay, well still. It should have ended there. I should never have allowed myself to—." I stopped talking, realizing what I was about to admit to someone other than myself.

"You fell for him," she said quietly, the laughter coming to a halt. "Oh, honey."

"It's fine," I lied. "Really. It's only been a few days. It's not like I'm in *love* with him. It's just the infatuation and excitement of something new. It'll pass as quickly as it came."

"Does he feel the same way?" she asked, ignoring my attempt to dismiss what had happened.

"He said he did earlier. I asked if it was too soon about us feeling this way about each other, and he assured me that when you know something is right, you don't fight it—or some shit like that."

My mind was swirling with thoughts of everything that had

happened today: Luke admitting that he had feelings for me; him confessing how I was so different from his family; his mom insinuating that I was a slut and slept with him to get the job (if only she knew that I slept with him *after* I got the job!). Then, there was the bombshell of meeting his wife.

"How did he act when you met his wife?"

"He was pissed that she was there and wasn't friendly to her at all. He even asked her *why* she was there. She said that his sister invited him."

"Do you think she would do that?"

"I don't know, honestly. I barely know him or his family. But his sister seems nice, so it doesn't seem like she would do it to piss him off—especially since he's responsible for making sure her wedding is perfect tomorrow. If anyone was that malicious, it's his mom."

"Maybe that's who invited her?"

"Who knows. She doesn't like me, but there hasn't been much time for her to sit around plotting this either. Unless she had it planned—."

I stopped what I was saying when it finally clicked.

"What? What did she have planned?"

"I bet you she planned to invite his wife all along. That's why she was so mad that he was there with me."

"That would make sense," Charlie agreed.

I heard a knock on my door and knew that I needed to talk to Luke at some point.

"Luke's at my door," I explained quietly in case he could hear me on the other side.

"Okay, text me later and let me know what happens."

I hung up and set my phone on the nightstand before checking myself in the mirror as I walked over to answer the door.

I pulled it open and found him on the other side, changed out of his dress attire and wearing a plain white t-shirt and gray sweats.

"I know that you're mad at me—and you have every reason to be, but can I please talk to you and explain what happened?"

"Luke, you don't need to," I sighed, leaning against the doorframe. "I wish you would have told me that you're married before anything happened between us, but we're past that now. So let's just move on and forget that anything even happened."

He closed his eyes and pulled his lips together in frustration.

"I'm not the kind of girl who gets involved with married men. It's my fault for not asking if you were married before anything happened, but I can guarantee that nothing will happen again."

I grabbed the door and started to close it when he stuck his hand out and held it open.

"Tiffany, I'm not married. We're separated and have been for five years. The only reason that we're not divorced is because she refuses to sign the papers."

"Why?"

"I don't have any freaking idea," he mumbled, running a hand through his hair. "She and my mom stayed friends after we split up, and I'm sure my mom has been the one convincing her not to sign, hoping that I'll give in and move back to Cedar Plank. She would love nothing more than to have me move back home and try to control my life like she does my sisters."

"Do you think that it was your mom that invited her to the wedding?"

"I can almost guarantee it."

I nodded and processed what he was saying. It made sense, and I wanted to believe him, but part of me felt like I needed to slap a handful of Band-Aids on my heart and get that wall up again before I ended up getting hurt.

"I'm sorry that I didn't tell you about her and that you had to find out the way that you did. June isn't someone that I like to talk about, and seeing her tonight just reminded me why I left home, to begin with."

"I didn't like finding out that way either," I replied bitterly. "But thank you for being honest with me and telling me what happened."

"You deserve to know the truth, and I'm sorry that I hurt you."

He turned and walked down the hall to the living room. I debated whether or not to chase after him. My heart begged my feet to start moving, but my head screamed for me to stop.

Fourteen

Tiffany

I stood there in awe, checking out the room where the ceremony would take place this afternoon. There were white folding chairs lined up in rows with an aisle down the middle that had a deep plum-colored runner leading to the altar at the front. Behind that was a floor-to-ceiling window that took up most of the wall, showcasing the perfect winter wonderland outside. Fresh snow had fallen, making it look light and fluffy against the dark evergreen trees that lined the back.

The altar had ropes of white Christmas lights strung throughout the wrought iron arched with a heart at the center. White roses were tucked into the structure and added to the soft romantic feeling in the room. Along the aisle were lanterns with tea lights that flickered shadows on the walls of the dimly lit room. I closed my eyes for a second and imagined what it would be like to have a wedding like this someday.

"It's beautiful, isn't it?" Julianna asked, coming to stand next to me.

"Gorgeous. I can't believe this is the same room. It looks so different from when I saw it the first time."

"Wait until you see the ballroom where they're having the reception. It's just as stunning. Luke does amazing work."

"I can see that," I laughed, feeling butterflies at the mention of his name. "I'd better get going, or we're not going to have a dinner to serve tonight," I joked, winking as I headed out.

I passed a few staff members on my way to the kitchen, saying hi and chatting for a few seconds as I walked. I loved that everyone was so nice and easy to work with. While I had no catering experience, I had expected it to be more of a challenge than it was. Going into someone's kitchen and taking over isn't usually met with the courtesy and respect I had been given from the start.

I spent the day working with Ernesto and his staff, getting ready for the big event. I was more nervous than anyone—probably even the bride. There was so much on the line that my palms had sweat so profusely that I worried I would lose my grip on the knife I was holding.

Just as I was about to cut into a tomato, I felt a hand slide around my waist and startle me. I dropped the knife before I cut my finger.

"Do I need to worry about you with a knife?" Luke asked, his voice low in my ear. His hand stayed on my side, spreading heat throughout me as I remembered the way it felt when it caressed my body this morning. Last night, I went to bed upset about what happened and woke up to him wanting to make it up to me.

"I'm starting to think that maybe I should stay away from them," I laughed, turning to face him. "Aren't you supposed to be getting ready for the wedding?" I asked, checking my watch. "It starts in an hour."

"Yeah, I'm heading that way now, but I wanted to stop in and say hi. I hate that you won't be there with me."

"Well, I would, but then no one would have anything to eat once it was over," I teased, bopping him on the nose with my finger.

"I know what I want to eat," he whispered in my ear with a growl.

I felt the heat spread further throughout my body, a slight ache starting between my thighs.

"If you keep talking like that, we're going to find ourselves in the same position we were in this morning," I giggled as his fingers dug into my sides and tickled.

"Well, I have to admit, it was a nice way to start Christmas Eve. You were the best present I found under the tree."

I hid my face in his neck, turning away as I had a vivid flashback of him going down on me in front of the Christmas tree while I was sprawled out on the plush shag rug. It was hard to believe that it was already Christmas Eve and that I wasn't spending the holiday with my family this year.

Then I thought about how happy I was this morning and how I didn't have to bother getting dressed up and making sure my makeup was perfect. Hell, I hadn't even bothered to put any on this morning, knowing that I would sweat it off in the kitchen. The expectations that usually followed me during the holidays were so far out of reach that I felt liberated for one in my life.

Luke gave me a quick kiss and headed off to the wedding while I tried to get my head straight and focus on the meal. A couple of hours later, the appetizers and side salads were being served, and I felt myself starting to relax, knowing that everything was running smoothly. The waitstaff was on point, delivering meals and grabbing hot plates before we could set them down. Dinner was out in record time with only a few stray plates that went out a few minutes delayed, and those were to the photographer and DJ who hadn't been at their table to eat right away anyway.

After the food was served, I tossed my hat and apron to the side and sat down on an empty crate. My feet hurt, and my back was achy. My job was officially done, and the kitchen would soon be handling the cake, which I had no desire to stick around for.

Just as I was getting cleaned up and changed, I heard Luke's voice in the kitchen. I smiled, knowing that he was waiting for me. When I walked out, I found him talking with Julianna, who was grinning from ear to ear.

"This is UNBELIEVABLE!" she exclaimed. "I can't wait to tell her!"

"Well, there she is," Luke said, nodding to me and smiling.

"What's going on?" I asked, feeling the excitement in the air.

"I was just telling Luke that thanks to Laney's recent posts about the wedding, we are already booked solid for weddings starting next September!"

"That's awesome, congratulations!" I said, not sure what this had to do with me.

"Laney shared pictures of the food that you served for the rehearsal dinner, and her posts have already gone viral!" Julianna added, her eyes wide.

"It was just basic bar food," I laughed, remembering how I tried to make it fancy by adding some garnishment to the buffet at the last minute before Ernesto stopped me.

"Not according to her and her new husband," she gushed. "They absolutely loved how you quote, *turned simple pub food into something extraordinary and worthy of a five-star restaurant.*" She used her fingers to end the quote.

"I don't do much on social media, but I'm guessing this is pretty big? Does she have a couple hundred followers or something?" I asked, completely clueless.

"My sister has a decent following and declined my parent's help paying for the wedding due to how padded her bank account is. They laughed when she told them she was going to be a social media influencer, but the joke is on them."

"Well, thanks to your sister, we are now on the map as the top destination for winter weddings next year. She's called it a Wonderland Wedding, and now everyone wants one!"

"That's great! I'm so happy for you guys."

"That's not the best part," Julianna said with a smirk growing across her face.

I narrowed my eyes and waited.

"The best part is that she gave you a glowing review as the caterer, and you've been personally requested for at least half of the weddings!"

"But I'm not a caterer," I stammered, looking to Luke for help. "I don't have a business set up or any supplies. I wouldn't have any idea how to get started, and honestly, I don't have the money—"

"That's why I would like to offer you a position at Bear Creek as our caterer. Now that we have a booked calendar next year, we need a caterer that we can rely on and that works well with our staff."

"You're offering me a job?" I asked in disbelief. There was no way this was real.

"I am. And I'm hoping that you'll say yes because I have a lot of brides that will be disappointed if you say no."

"But, I don't even live here."

"If you took the job, we would provide housing in the staff cabins. The monthly rent would be included in your salary package. What do you think?"

I looked at Luke, who was grinning with a proud smile.

"I think that I would love to work here. I accept!"

She gave me a quick hug and promised that we'd sit down after Christmas and go over the details. After she left and we were alone, he walked with me down the empty corridor to the reception hall.

"So, how do you feel about it?" he asked.

"Wonderful," I gushed, still feeling the high of it all. "I can't believe that I'm getting my dream job and the chance to start over."

I knew that we hadn't talked about it before now, but I hated that he was going back to LA. Would we even be able to make a long-distance relationship work?

"You deserve it, Tiffany."

"I'll miss you," I blurted out, stopping in my tracks. He reached out and held my hands, bringing them up to his lips to kiss them.

"Then I guess it's a good thing that I accepted her offer to become the exclusive wedding planner for Bear Creek."

I smiled and reached up to kiss him, knowing that he was the best gift I could have ever asked for.

Acknowledgments

Thank you to everyone that has taken the time to read this quick holiday novella. I hope it warmed your heart and gave you a quick little escape into a dreamy winter wonderland!

Just as my book was short and sweet, so are my acknowledgements.

Thank you Azucena and Chelsea for your help with this one. I appreciate you ladies! Tillie, thank you for taking the time to do edits for me, you're the best! Katy, Camille, and Amanda—thank you ladies so much for beta reading this for me and for giving me feedback!

I always appreciate the love and support that I get from my family and friends with each book I release and every adventure I embark upon. Thank you for always believing in me and pushing me to keep going.

To my loving husband and beautiful girls—thank you for letting me do something that I love and for cheering me on along the way. I love you more than you know!

If you've read my story and enjoyed it, please consider leaving a review to let other readers know. Nothing speaks louder than a happy reader, telling others about their great find!

Other Books By Samantha Baca

<u>The Haven Brook Series:</u>
'Til Death Do Us Part (Haven Brook Book 1)
https://books2read.com/u/m2RJNR

The Cradle Will Fall (Haven Brook Book 2)
https://books2read.com/u/b6O0QE

The Ties That Bind (Haven Brook Book 3)
https://books2read.com/u/mqgoz8

A Very Haven Christmas (Haven Brook Book 4- Novella)
https://books2read.com/u/mvqGjj

Three Strikes, You're Gone (Haven Brook Book 5)
https://books2read.com/u/mvqL2z
****

<u>The Dark Shadows Series</u>
Five Steps Ahead (Dark Shadows Book 1)
https://books2read.com/u/38Q0gO

****

The Stone Creek Series (Novellas)
Chocolate Covered Mistletoe (Stone Creek Book 1)
https://books2read.com/u/3LRk9N

Candy Coated Promises (Stone Creek Book 2)
https://books2read.com/u/mldP5Y

Pumpkin Spiced Possibilities (Stone Creek Book 3)
https://books2read.com/u/bojdwV
****

Stand-Alone Books
One Last Wish
https://books2read.com/u/mqg7D9

Finding Love In Apartment 2C (Novella)
https://books2read.com/u/bze9aZ

Cocky Counsel: A Hero Club Novel
https://www.amazon.com/Cocky-Counsel-Hero-Club-Novel-ebook/dp/B09GG4MR5M/

About the Author

Samantha lives in the southwest with her husband and two small children after abandoning her childhood dream of living in a cabin in Colorado when she found that she couldn't afford to live there and was deathly allergic to the woods. When she's not writing she's usually spouting off sarcastic remarks while drinking wine out of a coffee mug to look like a functional adult while chasing down her toddlers. She enjoys spending time with her family, watching reruns of Friends, and the 24/7 flow of coffee that can be found in her veins. Be sure to follow her on social media for updates on what she's working on.

You can find her here:

Facebook: https://www.facebook.com/AuthorSamanthaBaca

Instagram: https://instagram.com/author_samantha_baca

Goodreads: http://www.goodreads.com/authorsamanthabaca

Facebook Reader Group:

https://www.facebook.com/groups/2945710968775398/

Webpage: https://authorsamanthabaca.wordpress.com

Newsletter: http://eepurl.com/g0NcSj